W9-CAT-175

This book is dedicated to the memory of Judy Hammond, a colleague who unknowingly ignited the spark that started my own practice of gratitude and this story.

Before I Sleep

I Say Thank You

Written by Carol Gordon Ekster

Illustrated by Mary Rojas

BOOKS & MEDIA
Boston

Library of Congress Cataloging-in-Publication Data

Ekster, Carol Gordon.
Before I sleep I say thank you / written by Carol Gordon Ekster ; illustrated by Mary Rojas.
pages cm
Summary: At bedtime, a mother and child think about their day and remember one thing each is sorry for, then the child recalls five things to be grateful for, takes a peaceful breath, and falls asleep. Includes notes for children and adults.
ISBN 978-0-8198-1225-4 -- ISBN 0-8198-1225-0
[1. Bedtime--Fiction. 2. Prayer--Fiction. 3. Mother and child--Fiction.] I. Rojas, Mary, illustrator. II. Title.
PZ7.E3478Bef 2015
[E]--dc23
2014004606

This is a work of fiction. Names, characters, places, events, and incidents are either the products of the author's imagination or used in a fictitious manner. Any resemblance to actual persons, living or dead, or actual events is purely coincidental.

Book design by Mary Joseph Peterson, FSP

Cover art and illustrations by Mary Rojas

Published by Pauline Books & Media, 50 Saint Pauls Avenue, Boston, MA 02130–3491

Printed in Korea

BIS SIPSKOGUNKYO4-30067 1225-0

www.pauline.org

Pauline Books & Media is the publishing house of the Daughters of St. Paul, an international congregation of women religious serving the Church with the communications media.

4 5 6 7 8 9 22 21 20 19 18

For Grown-ups

"Saying prayers" before sleep is part of many children's bedtime routine. This might include some traditional prayers, like the Lord's Prayer, or a list of "God bless __________ (name of person)." Those are valid ways to pray; this book suggests another option.

Saint Ignatius of Loyola introduced the *Examen* prayer, a prayer of the heart. It offers a method for reviewing the day and experiencing how God is present throughout that day. This review is a way of both acknowledging one's shortcomings and recognizing God's love and blessings. Saint Ignatius believed that expressing gratitude for God's presence in our lives and his many gifts was the single most important practice of spirituality.

This book shares a simplified way for children to practice Saint Ignatius's *Examen* prayer: Quietly reflect on the day for a minute or two. With small children a minute is plenty of time. Take note of shortcomings or missed opportunities, things you wish you had done differently. Share them with God and tell him you are sorry. Ask for God's grace to do better in the future. Recognize God's blessings and gifts received throughout the day. Share five of them to let God know you are grateful.

However you adapt this method, our hope is that it enables your child to share his or her wonder and joy in this amazing world and that your family reaps the benefit of this beautiful practice.

Tuck-in time is my favorite part of the day. Tonight, it's Mommy's turn.

"Almost done brushing," I mumble with a mouthful of minty toothpaste.

Mommy clasps her hands behind her and I hook on to them. She's the train and I'm the caboose.

"Choo-choo!" we chant as we chug to my room.

"Again?" I ask. Some nights I get another ride. Other times Mommy says, "Sorry, Honey." But tonight I get a surprise.

"How about a plane ride instead?" she asks. Our arms stretch into wings. And we fly!

Now it's really time for bed. Mommy clicks on the night-light. I hop up and slide between the sheets. She tucks the blanket around me, brushes my hair with her hand, and asks, "Are you cozy-comfortable?"

I nod my head and we begin our goodnight prayers.

Mommy whispers, "Let's take a moment to think about our day." She takes my hands in hers and we close our eyes.

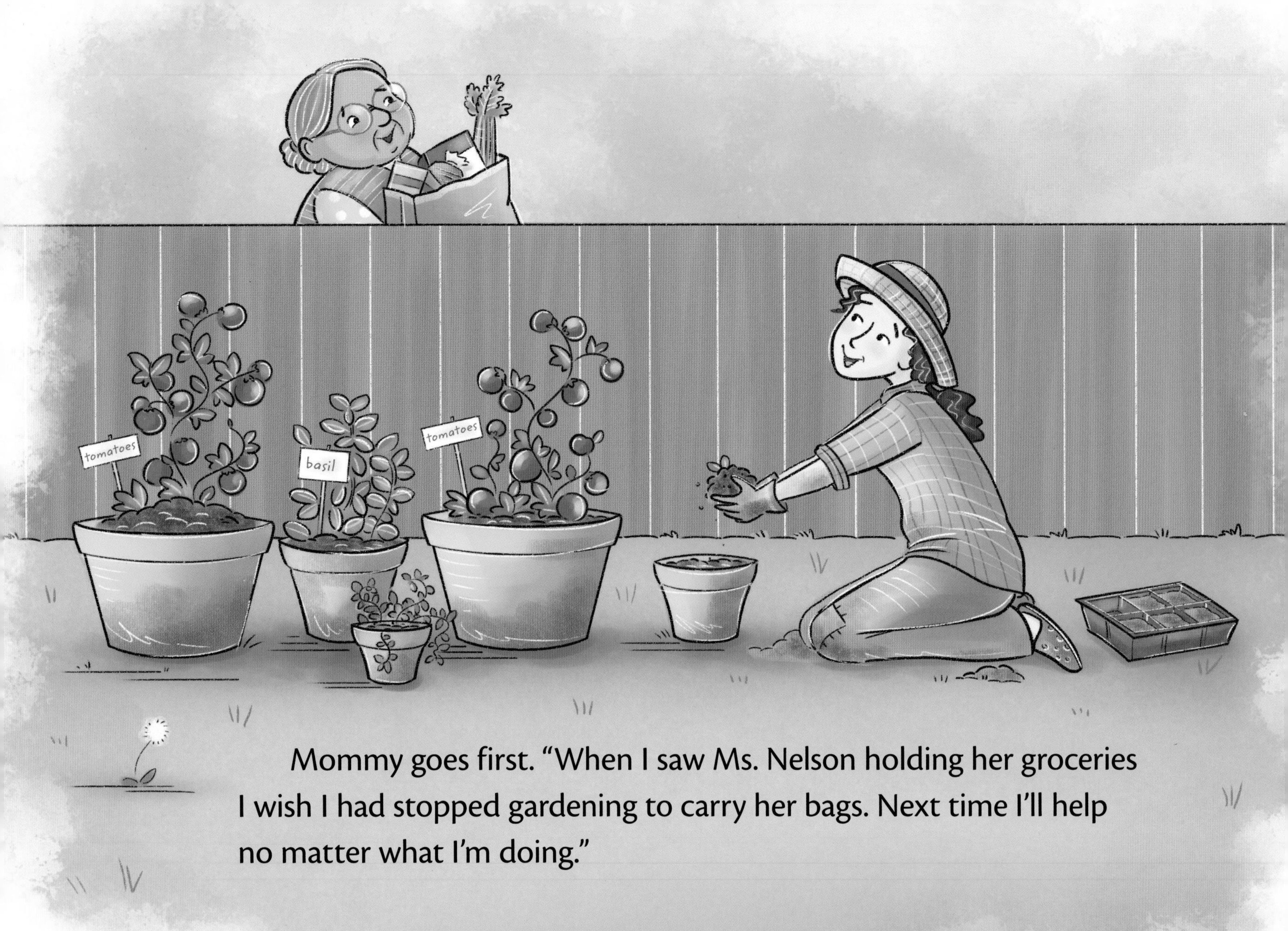

Mommy goes first. "When I saw Ms. Nelson holding her groceries I wish I had stopped gardening to carry her bags. Next time I'll help no matter what I'm doing."

Now it's my turn.
"I'm sorry I didn't pick tomatoes with you when you asked. Tomorrow I promise I'll cooperate all day long!"

I get a ten-second hug. "Thank you, Sweetheart. And for our blessings? I really appreciated you setting the table tonight. What five things do you thank God for?"

"Daddy reading me a story. We cuddled on the couch with my favorite book, and Jet, too!"

Jet jumps up to say goodnight. He knows I was talking about him. I nuzzle my nose against his. He scoots off, tickling me with his tail. He's not ready for bed yet.

“I’m grateful Danny shared his snack with me, apple slices dipped in sticky honey. Can I bring that for snack sometime?”

“We’ll see,” she answers, asking me with her eyes to continue.

"And then at recess the big kids let me play soccer with them and I scored!"

My eyes blink with sleepiness but I keep thinking about my day.

"I'm grateful I caught the perfect frog. But I let him go so he could find his friends."

In a voice as quiet as a secret Mommy says, "One more."
I answer, "You tucking me in."

Then together we say, "Thank you, God, for all you have given us today."

Mommy sings our goodnight song, then kisses my forehead.

She waits for me to take my "peaceful breath." Before I sleep I take a deep breath, bringing "peace-" inside me. Then I breathe out "-ful," with a whoosh of air to send peace out to everyone everywhere so the whole world is full of peace. I've done this every night since I was little.

When the door clicks shut, I snuggle my pillow. Pictures of other things I'm grateful for parade across my eyes like a movie. And the last one is . . .

sleep.

Now it's your turn!

Can you think of something you wish you had done differently? Tell God you are sorry.

And what five things are *you* grateful for?

Here are some suggestions:

. . . the sweet sound of music.

. . . my family.

. . . silky flower petals with their perfumy smell.

. . . feeling healthy today.

. . . my friends.

. . . my teacher.

. . . school.

. . . food.

. . . books.

Thank you, God,
for all your gifts!

Carol Gordon Ekster

When not working on her books, Carol spends time doing yoga, reading, and bike riding. She is the author of *Where Am I Sleeping Tonight? (A Story of Divorce)* and *Ruth the Sleuth and the Messy Room*. Carol Gordon Ekster was a passionate elementary school teacher for thirty-five years. Now retired, Carol is grateful that her writing allows her to continue communicating with children. She lives in Andover, MA, with her husband, Mark.

Mary Rojas

Mary Rojas has been a freelance illustrator for more than ten years. Her work is joyfully colorful and often whimsical. Mary has illustrated many children's educational texts and storybooks for a wide variety of publishers. Her first Pauline Kids picture book, *Forever You: A Book About Your Soul and Body,* won a Christopher Award. *Before I Sleep* is her second collaboration with Pauline Books & Media. Mary lives in San Antonio, TX, with her husband and son.

The Daughters of St. Paul operate book and media centers at the following addresses. Visit, call, or write the one nearest you today, or find us at www.pauline.org.

CALIFORNIA
3908 Sepulveda Blvd, Culver City, CA 90230 — 310-397-8676
3250 Middlefield Road, Menlo Park, CA 94025 — 650-369-4230

FLORIDA
145 S.W. 107th Avenue, Miami, FL 33174 — 305-559-6715

HAWAII
1143 Bishop Street, Honolulu, HI 96813 — 808-521-2731

ILLINOIS
172 North Michigan Avenue, Chicago, IL 60601 — 312-346-4228

LOUISIANA
4403 Veterans Memorial Blvd, Metairie, LA 70006 — 504-887-7631

MASSACHUSETTS
885 Providence Hwy, Dedham, MA 02026 — 781-326-5385

MISSOURI
9804 Watson Road, St. Louis, MO 63126 — 314-965-3512

NEW YORK
115 E. 29th Street, New York City, NY 10016 — 212-754-1110

SOUTH CAROLINA
243 King Street, Charleston, SC 29401 — 843-577-0175

TEXAS
No book center; for parish exhibits or outreach evangelization, contact: 210-569-0500, or SanAntonio@paulinemedia.com, or P.O. Box 761416, San Antonio, TX 78245

VIRGINIA
1025 King Street, Alexandria, VA 22314 — 703-549-3806

CANADA
3022 Dufferin Street, Toronto, ON M6B 3T5 — 416-781-9131

SMILE! God loves you.